Stories You Love

Aladdin

Retold by Gill Davies
Illustrated by Eric Kincaid

MECRON

Aladdin was a tailor's son who lived long a
in a Persian city. His father had long since
died. Aladdin and his mother were very po

Aladdin liked to play in the market where t
oranges were as **round** as golden suns an
the **oval** eggs as white as the moon.

ometimes, when he was hungry, Aladdin
as tempted to steal some food for supper.

stead, he would beg the fruit sellers to give
m fruits that were old or damaged. So at
ast he and his mother did not starve.

Princess Jasmine, who lived in the palace nearby, led a very different life. She was ric and could eat as much food as she liked.

Every day servants would present her with grapes piled high on **round** silver plates an big **square** boxes, overflowing with deliciou sweets.

hough she was never hungry, Princess
smine was unhappy. She was lonely. She
nged to play outside with the other young
ople of the city.

is was not allowed, of course. And soon she
ust marry. "We shall find you a rich husband
th many palaces," her father told her.

One day, when Aladdin was playing hide and seek in the market, a tall man arrived. He had a long nose, shaped like a **hook**.

This was a wicked magician but he pretended to be Aladdin's Uncle Ebeneezer.

ncle Ebeneezer' insisted on buying Aladdin
w clothes. He also bought five baskets,
imming over with good food. Then he asked
addin to take him to Aladdin's home.

addin's mother was grateful for the
nderful food the magician had brought her.
e made them all a delicious supper.

"I wish to take Aladdin with me on a long journey," said Uncle Ebeneezer. Aladdin thought this sounded very exciting. The next day Aladdin and his wicked uncle set off.

They went out through the city walls and the great stone **arches**.

hen they walked many miles till they
ached the pointed mountains that stood
ut like huge **triangles** against the sky.

p and over the mountains they went, until
ey arrived at an enormous cave.

low I need your help," said the magician.

"This is a magic place," he explained, "But the entrance to the cave is narrow. Only a thin boy like you can squeeze inside."

"Perhaps I should not have let you eat so much supper last night." He laughed.

Now in you go, Aladdin. You will see many
jewels and rich treasure inside. Do not touch
these. Just bring me the old lamp you will
see in the furthest corner."

Feeling a little nervous, Aladdin squeezed
through the long **cylinder**-shaped entrance
to the cave. He wriggled along on his tummy.

Then he stood up and gazed around him.
This was indeed a wonderful place. The
cave was full of treasures.

There was gold in abundance, rubies and
emeralds glinting in the shadows and huge
diamonds. These sparkled so brightly they
filled the cave with dancing patterns.

Aladdin popped some of these gems and a beautiful ring into his pockets.

"Can you see the lamp?" the magician called.

"Yes," shouted Aladdin. "Quickly! Quickly! Fetch it to me now," the magician shouted.

Aladdin picked up the old lamp.

"Pass the lamp to me now," the magician demanded. Suddenly Aladdin was afraid. He did not understand why the lamp was so important.

But he felt that the magician would not let him out of the cave once he had the lamp. "No," said Aladdin, "Wait until I am out."

The magician was furious. Three times he asked Aladdin to pass him the lamp and three times Aladdin refused, moving further back into the cave.

In a sudden burst of anger the magician waved his magic wand. A great **round** stone rolled over the entrance. Aladdin was trapped.

Aladdin was very frightened. He heard
the magician screeching outside and then
a loud sound as he flew far away, over the
mountains on a magic carpet. "Now what c
I to do?" Aladdin wondered.

He sat down. "This is a very dirty lamp," he
said, rubbing it to see if it was gold beneath
the dust.

Then his mother suddenly remembered, "You still have the magic ring. That can grant wishes too." At once Aladdin fetched the ring. "Bring Princess Jasmine back, please, please, oh Ring," begged Aladdin.

In an instant, the palace and the Princess appeared before him. She had the magic lamp.

In a flash, the evil man asked the genie of the lamp to take the palace and Princess to his secret place in the desert, where Aladdin would never find them again.

When Aladdin discovered what had happened, he was broken-hearted.

Now Aladdin had never told Princess
Jasmine about the magic lamp and genie.
So when the magician appeared outside
Aladdin's palace crying, "New lamps for old!
New lamps for old!" Jasmine thought,
"Aladdin would like a new lamp."

She fetched the old lamp from the **round**
tower and gave it to the wicked magician.

The Sultan was very impressed with Aladdin's gifts and with Aladdin's wonderful palace.

So, much to the Princess's delight, the Sultan said, "Yes, you may marry each other." They were very happily married.

Now for a long time Aladdin had admired the pretty Princess. He had never dared hope to meet her for he was only a poor tailor's son. Now, he was the richest young man in Persia.

He sent Princess Jasmine the loveliest jewels from the cave and asked the Sultan for permission to marry his beautiful daughter.

Aladdin asked for a splendid palace and there it was, the richest palace in the world with round **domes**, tall **towers** and gardens with long **rectangular** lawns and rose **arches**.

It did not take Aladdin long to say, "Please, Genie, will you take me home?" The genie did this straight away.

Now, Aladdin and his mother were rich. Aladdin's pockets were full of dazzling jewels. Moreover, the genie could provide them with everything they needed. The beautiful ring turned out to be magic too.

There was a sudden flash of brilliant light and a **spiralling swirl** of green smoke.

A genie shot into the air. "I am the Genie of the Lamp," boomed the voice, "Your wish is my command, oh, Master."